Contents

The martial arts

Martial arts are exciting sports where you fight **opponents** one-on-one.

In many martial arts, the aim is to strike your opponent with your hands or feet.

OPPONENT
a person who is on the opposite side in a game

4

FIRST SPORT

MARTIAL ARTS

James Nixon

Photography by Bobby Humphrey

W

FRANKLIN WATTS

LONDON • SYDNEY

Franklin Watts
First published in Great Britain in 2016
by The Watts Publishing Group

Series Editor: Julia Bird
Planning and production by Discovery Books Ltd
Editor: James Nixon
Series designer: Ian Winton

Commissioned photography: Bobby Humphrey
Picture credits: Shutterstock: pp. 2 (Lucian Coman),
3 (Apollofoto), 4 (Pavel L Photo and Video),
6 (PhotoStock10), 7 top (joyfull), 7 bottom (Luis Louro),
13 bottom (Ilya Andriyanov), 15 top (Attl Tibor), 19 (testing).

The author, packager and publisher would like to thank
Bradford Judo Club: www.bradfordjudoclub.co.uk;
Leeds Karate Academy: www.lka.org.uk; and
NTX Taekwondo Schools: www.ntx-schools.net,
for their help and participation in this book.

Dewey number: 796.8
ISBN: 978 1445 1 4905 9
Library ebook ISBN: 978 1445 1 2635 7

Printed in China

Franklin Watts
An imprint of Hachette Children's Group
Part of The Watts Publishing Group
Carmelite House, 50 Victoria Embankment, London EC4Y 0DZ

An Hachette UK Company
www.hachette.co.uk

www.franklinwatts.co.uk

MIX
Paper from
responsible sources
FSC® C104740
FSC
www.fsc.org

In other martial arts, opponents **grapple** with each other. Lots of people do martial arts to get fit and to learn ways to defend themselves.

GRAPPLE
a fight where opponents grip each other

Judo

In judo you have to grapple with your opponent. The aim is to throw them to the floor. The better the throw, the more points you score.

ROU
ESP

D.RAMIREZ

RAMIRE

-66 kg 3 13

If your opponent lands on their back, the match ends and you win!

Judo matches last up to five minutes and take place on a mat. This stops players hurting themselves when they fall.

The only kit you need is an outfit called a **judogi**, which is tied at the waist with a belt.

JUDOGI the cotton jacket and trousers worn in a judo match

Judo: throws and trips

There are many different judo throws. A player can use their hips (left) or legs (below) to lift their opponent up and throw them onto the mat.

An important skill in judo is to make your moves at the right time. If you wait until your opponent is **off-balance**, you can then trip them to the floor with your leg.

OFF-BALANCE
not balanced and at risk of being knocked over

Judo: groundwork

Judo players often end up grappling on the ground. A clever move is to drop down onto your back and throw your opponent over with your legs.

On the ground a player can try to **pin** their opponent down.

PIN
hold someone down firmly so they are unable to move

If you can hold down your opponent in the same position for 25 seconds, you win.

Karate

In karate points are scored for landing different punches and kicks.

The most difficult attacks, such as this high kick, score three points.

In **sparring** exercises you practise moves against a partner without using force. Shields are used in training so that you can practise kicks and punches.

SPARRING carrying out fighting moves without making strong contact

For competition you will need guards for your head and mouth, and **mitts** to cover your fists.

MITT a padded glove used in fighting sports for safety

Karate: punching and kicking

Punching is the most important skill in karate. Punches should be made with a straight arm and travel from your hip towards the target.

There are many kicks to learn. A front kick is fast and can push an opponent back.

By spinning on one foot, you can kick powerfully with your other foot sideways and backwards.

Karate: blocking

Defending is just as important as attacking in martial arts. In karate punches can be blocked with the back or front of your hand.

You can use your arms to block high or low punches and kicks.

You also need fast **footwork** to win a karate match. It helps you to dodge attacks and hit your opponent.

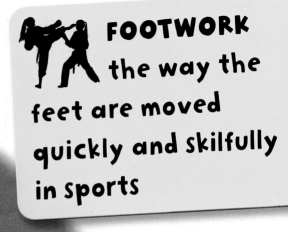

FOOTWORK the way the feet are moved quickly and skilfully in sports

17

Taekwondo

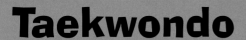

The name taekwondo means 'way of the foot and the fist'.

Taekwondo is best known for the amazing, jumping kicks that players perform on each other.

In a taekwondo match, players wear guards on their chest and head. These guards have coloured target areas on them. To score points you must hit the targets on your opponent.

Taekwondo: ready to fight

The first thing to learn in taekwondo is how to stand. Being in the correct position makes it easier for you to attack with punches and kicks.

The fighting **stances** that you learn also put you in the perfect position to defend.

To stop your opponent from scoring you can block with your legs, as well as your hands and arms.

21

Taekwondo: flying kicks

In taekwondo kicks are more useful than punches. Legs can reach further than arms and are more likely to find the target.

All kicks begin with a bent knee. Then the leg is **thrust** out suddenly with power.

THRUST to push forwards quickly with force

With a short run-up, spectacular flying kicks can be carried out with both feet off the floor.

Index